Titles by *l*

Chopchair

Linus T. Asong

Langaa Research & Publishing CIG
Mankon, Bamenda

Publisher:
Langaa RPCIG
Langaa Research & Publishing Common Initiative Group
P.O. Box 902 Mankon
Bamenda
North West Region
Cameroon
Langaagrp@gmail.com
www.langaa-rpcig.net

Distributed outside N. America by African Books
Collective
orders@africanbookscollective.com
www.africanbookscollective.com

Distributed in N. America by Michigan State
University Press
msupress@msu.edu
www.msupress.msu.edu

ISBN: 9956-616-13-3

DISCLAIMER

The names, characters, places and incidents in this book are either the product of the author's imagination or are used fictitiously. Accordingly, any resemblance to actual persons, living or dead, events, or locales is entirely one of incredible coincidence.

Contents

Part One

Part Two

Part Three

Part One

When I have one foot in the grave I will tell
the truth about women. I shall tell it, jump into
my coffin, pull the lid over me, and say,
"Do you what you like now."
(TOLSTOY)

Chapter One

"I need a Chopchair, Nkem," Fuo Akendong II said resolutely but desperately. Although he was looking only into Eshuo- Fuo's eyes, he saw addressing Michael Nkem Fou and Nicodemus Eshou- Fuo, his two closest associates in the inner council of the palace of Betaranda in Lewoh.

The man on whom he pinned his eyes was the palace sage. His name was Ndi Nkem-Fuo. Ndi Michael Nkem-Fuo was full 11 years older than the chief himself. His people call him "Mackay, "or simply "Ndi Ma." In spite of the respect he commanded in the palace, he was universally known as a man of extremely filthy habits. He was a great snuff taker who never cared to clean his nose or carry a handkerchief for that purpose, cleared his throat and spat at will. His breath stank foully (more from a natural defect than the snuff), and it was even said that he was never ashamed of urinating in front of women at the market place. Something of an abomination!

His teeth were badly disfigured, he ate heavily (disparagingly, some called him chop-die!), and he always wore a small home-made *jumpa* which exposed his thin arms and bony chest. He wore a "country cap" and rubber shoes (of which it was said he never took off, not even when he bathed or went to bed).

Mackay Eshuo-Fuo was just about the same age with Nkem-Fuo. A tallish lean and hungry looking old man who spent most of his waking hours drinking palm wine and locally brewed gin. Because of an accident in his infancy, he usually carried a walking stick which he personally embroidered. He was small in stature, his hands skinny and even bony, his fingers nimble and he had small eyes that glittered below his hooded eye-brows like a diamond in the dark.

Though his physical appearance was generally repulsive, he had some redeeming elements: vivacious and endlessly entertaining, he had a strong sense of humour that the villagers appreciated. This however was not easily noticeable when he was the company of the Chief because the latter was naturally a man of very severe disposition. His company was always in high demand. One thing bound him to the Chief: his undying loyalty as well as the fact that he never contradicted the Chief, even when he knew the Chief was in the wrong.

The second man was Nichodemus Eshuo-Fuo. People scarcely ever called him Nichodemus because the name was rather too long. They always addressed him "Mbe Eshuo-Fuo." He was older than Nkem-Fuo by at least ten years, but he was a more attractive human being. Unlike Nkem-Fuo who had tried very unsuccessfully to blacken his hair with shoe polish, he left his hair as it was – thick, grey. During any public ceremony, his head gear was a topic of discussion: it rose in folds over his head, each fold carrying tassels of different colours, and ended up in a bunch of multicoloured feathers which many thought he should have given to the Chief.

He was very light in complexion, a fact which was accentuated by the whiteness of the hairs on his arms and chest. The hair from his head ran in a carefully trimmed bunch round his chin and over his upper lip. He did not talk much, though it was obvious that he was a much mire brilliant man than his friend, Eshuonti. He behaved rather snobbishly towards the villagers, and usually preferred to keep his opinions to himself. When he chose to speak, though, his views were invariably worth listening to.

4

These two men were entirely dependent on the judgement of the Chief for their pleasure, necessities and even their lives.

***

It was as though the very words would cause God to grant his wish. Ndi Nkem-Fuo nodded silently. After a moment he said rather hesitantly: "I think Achiebio does. Or what do you think?" he turned ho his mate.

"Is it something to ask again?" the second man said. They were used to liking only what the chief liked and hating only the things he hated. "Of course," Mackay Eshuo-Fuo repeated. "If Achiebio does not have a Chopchair, who then should?" In their hearts, and sometimes when they were together in the absence of the Chief, the two men had often wondered why the Chief could not forget about it and make one of the four sons he had with his first wife his Chopchair. But then, they would recall that the Chief, having expelled the woman on a slight and doubtful charge of infidelity, had disowned all the four boys who now lived in the palace like strangers.

There was a time when the Chief had about ten nobles of his age to attend to him. But over the years, the pressures of poverty brought about by the Chief's continuous efforts to live high and extravagant life, coupled with his inability to seek or listen to advice from his so-called advisers coursed him to sell titles of Sub-Chiefs to most of the old men. These were only too happy to live independently and establish their separate small kingdoms.

Neither Mackay Eshuo-Fuo nor Nichodemus Nkem-Fuo were ambitious to the extent of wanting to live apart from the Chief. Nobody ever called Nichodemus by his first name. They found it too difficult to pronounce. Quite unlike the Chief, the two men were in no need of Chopchairs, because they each had at least three sons. Apart from the fact that they were not so ambitious as to pose a threat to the Chief's power, they were neither rich nor strong enough to live on their own. They preferred to live off the generosity of the Chief.

***

A long silence fell after Eshuo concurred the second time. The hulking Chieftain strode forth and back flexing and unflexing his muscles, gnawing viciously at his lower lip, blinking his eyes as though the wind had blown some strange objects into them.

Nkem-Fuo studied him carefully for the one millionth time. He stood close to two meters, or could actually be two meters and more and weighed over 110 kilograms. As ever, the face was unsmiling and there was the perpetual frown on his fore head gear which bore his bunch of hair like a sack and virtually rested on his left shoulder. His thick sideburns linked to his thick moustache with a clean shaven chin, gave a comic dimension to another wise permanently severe countenance.

As his habit was when he was relaxing at home in the afternoon, he was shirtless. His massive chest and belly sprayed with strands and patches of grey and black hairs rose and fell. The hair began from under his chin and descended into the folds of the loin cloth just below his navel. He was wearing his home-made over-sized rubber slippers displaying longish, finger-like toes with nails that had grown and curved over the toes into the floor of the slippers

Chapter Two

The whole world was alive. It was only three o'clock in the afternoon, but frogs could be heard croaking in the fish pond down behind the palace garden. A sheep bleated, a cock had been crowing for the past hour, pigs groaned and wallowed in the mud, bees hummed round the flowers in the papaw trees, sun birds chirped noisily cheerfully, flew from one flower to the other. Two of the five scrawny dogs that guarded the palace lay restlessly at the entrance into the Chief's sitting room, one on each side of the entrance, both wagging their tails, shaking their bleeding ears to send flies away.

Nor was it a problem for the animals alone. The Chief and his noble each held a small broom with which they drove, struck, and sometimes killed the flies that swarmed down on their sweating bodies as though there were in a slaughterhouse. Since this was the moment to cut grass, till the soil in readiness for planting, the smell of burning grass, elephants stalks and dried leaves was very much in the air,.

***

Taking Nkem-Fuo by the hand and with Eshuo-Fuo following, Fuo Akendong led them into his sitting room area which Mackay once described as having the richness and variety of a medicine man's shrine.

"You cannot hide excreta from the anus," the chief said. "I want to see the thorns on which I am walking," he said, beckoning to them, his eyes turning more and more red with desperation. "I want you two who are my remaining shadows to see the prickly thorns on which I lie." He showed Nkem-Fuo his dane gun, five spears, mortars, wooden spoons, masks, brass statues of snakes, lizards, birds and many other animals.

"These hands of mine, they made them all," he added significantly, striking his chest proudly with both hands. He showed the old man a collection of stuffed animals: an eagle, a hare, a hyena, a civet cat, a fox, an antelope, an owl and a pangolin.

"These hands made them all," he said showing them his large, wide open palms again.

The old men made no comment. These were all familiar objects to them. It was the significance the Chief was imparting on them that worried them.

Fuo Akendong pointed to a large green bottle on an old shelf. Its contents were amazing: a tightly bound bundle of sticks stood in it filling it to the neck as if the bottle had been built over the bundle. There was no way of telling how the bundle could have been inserted into it. There was another bottle close to it with contents that were just as baffling: eight eggs and more were carefully piled in it as though it were a plastic bag meant for the purpose. How on earth the eggs got in there through the small mouth of the bottle it was impossible to imagine.

"I made that too, myself," the Chief announced. Nkem –Fuo nodded. He knew all that too. The Chief took a drinking glass from his cupboard and chewed half of it and swallowed the pieces as if they were kola nuts or ground nuts.

The old men creaked in their joints, ground their toothless gums as the Chief performed the miracle. In fact, had they been strangers, they would have expected the Chief to drop dead any minute. But that was not to be. He had heard terrible tales told about this Chief.

Chapter Three

Fuo Akendong II did not stop there. There were a few more tricks in the bag! He held his palm, shook his jaws the way rabbits do, spat a good quantity of spittle in it and asked the two men to look at it carefully.

The spittle suddenly reappeared at the back of the palm without the men seeing how it happened. Fuo Akendong turned the back of his hand, the spittle now returned to the palm which was still facing downwards, not a drop fell down.

Fuo Akendong shook the spittle away and cleaned his large palm on his loin cloth. He took a handkerchief, opened it out and made it stand on its thin edge as though it was a piece of wood. He took three eggs and, making one stand on the small end, placed the second in like manner, and then the third until each egg stood on the other.

Nkem-Fuo knew how difficult it was to make just a single egg stand on either end on a hard surface, be it the big or small end. He struck his hands in endless wonder. Stories he had heard of the man's mysterious feats were legion. Mackay Eshuo-Fuo once told Nkem-Fuo one incident which fascinated him, which he personally witnessed in the market.

Soon after drinking from a glass which he chewed and swallowed, Fuo Akendong asked a woman who had come to sell palm wine to preserve a twenty litre jug for him. Towards the end of the day the woman as anxious to return to her village. She came up to him and asked him to empty the wine into his own container so that she could go away with her jug. Fuo Akendong is said to pour the drink into his hands which formed a funnel leading into his mouth.

The woman did. When to her greatest dismay it looked like the man would drink the entire twenty litres of wine, she was said to have dropped the jug and fled in fright.

"How does Fuo manage to do all this?" he enquired.

The Chief did not answer. Instead he pulled his head gear, exposing locks of hair that could quite easily have reached down to his waist if stretched.

"Perhaps you do not know that neither a knife nor a blade has ever touched a hair on my head," he said. "Nkem, I want you to know why I am disturbed," he said regretfully. "Do you know that if I die without a Chopchair, all this art will die with me?"

Nkem-Fuo grunted.

"There are certain things that only a man can do," he declared. "Ours is not a woman's world. This is not something you can hand over to a woman. Not with all the smoke in the air. A white cock that ins not conscious of its colour will surely rub palm oil on its back some day."

The old men nodded. "Achiebio is right," he said softly. They returned to the veranda.

"Those who don not understand the language of a dance think it is noise that is being made," he began. And then he lowered his voice: "Fourteen girls without a Chopchair are fourteen curses. Fourteen wounds. Fourteen daggers pointing at my heart," he screamed, clenched his fists and struck them together. "If Ngwika does not give me a boy today," he warned, "I will ask God to give the next pregnancy let me carry it myself and I will see whether I will not deliver a boy."

"Hmm," the old man grunted. The Chief strode to his lounge chair and threw himself into it. He pulled the foot rest, made it stand between his thighs and, supporting his head in his right hand began:

"I see treachery all over the place. People, who were supposed to serve me, are now waiting for me to die so that they prey on my kingdom. I see every single one of them charging in here to carry his own piece away. Just where did I go wrong?" he queried.

"I cannot see where Achiebo went wrong," Eshuo-Fuo said insincerely, inwardly cursing himself. If he could honestly voice an opinion about the Chief he would have said:

"Achiebio, the fault was yours. when Akeu-Mbin, Lebe, Ale-esoa and Bekoh each came to you with monies to buy the titles of Fuo, we tried to warn you that each of them to which you will give the title of Fuo will take a piece or you title away. We warned Achiebio that he derived his honour from the fact that these people were his servants and he should not allow them to claim even remotely that they were his equals. Now you are left alone. You cannot call a clean-up campaign and invite them because they have their own palaces to take care of."

But Nkem-Fuo said no such thing. He knew better than anybody else the obvious risk of drawing attention to what may be interpreted as a mistake on the part of the Chief. It was worse than putting one's finger into a fire.

Chapter Four

The suspense did not last long! While he was displaying his magic, and unknown to them, a stranger, a woman had made her way secretly through the palace gate and was waiting for a moment of silence to show her face. She knew that Fuo Akendong hated being interrupted. As soon as there was a pause in the conversation, she cleared her throat to draw attention.

"Who is there?" Fuo Akendong barked.

"Me, Achiebio," she said cowering towards the Chief. She was bringing news. She had travelled all day from the Health Centre at Lemvoah where the Chief's fifth wife had gone to deliver her first baby. The ghost of a smile played at the corners of the Chief's mouth.

***

"Tell me what I want to hear," he said impatiently. "Don't tell me that Ngwika has not delivered my Chopchair. Nkem," he turned to Eshuo-Fuo.

"Achiebio," the old man answered, praying with all his heart that the news should be what they really wanted to hear.

There was an elusive smile on the woman's face which implied that he was not bad news she was bringing after all.

"Achiebo will have cause to celebrate today," the messenger said, herself beaming with delight. "There is in fact, good news," she emphasised to remove any further lingering doubts from the Chief's mind.

True to his impulsive nature, Fuo-Akendong did not listen for the rest of the story. "When a true son of the soil speaks," he said striking his thighs with wild excitement, "the soil listens." He resumed his seat, and immediately threw his right hand over the arm of the chair and under the right side. When it returned it was clasping the small raffia bag that usually carried the drinking horn which he carved himself from camwood.

Eshuo-Fuo knew what the Chief expected was to happen next. He rose briskly entered the house and immediately came back with a calabash of fresh palm wine.

Fuo held out his horn which Nkem filled to the brim. Instead of drinking it he held it to Nkem-Fuo.

"Taste it, you Satans. I don't trust anybody any more."

"Even these old bones, Achiebio?"

"Taste it," he ordered. Most respectfully, Nkem-Fuo lifted the horn in both hands to his lips and then allowed Fuo-Akendong to take it back. The chieftain withdrew and then holding it to his own mouth drained the horn in one go.

"The fangs of a dead snake are just as deadly as those of the living. You think if I leave these my young women you will not..."

He interrupted himself when his eyes fell on Nkem-Fuo's troubled countenance and for once, he quickly tried to make amends. "Just joking," he said. The old man knew that the Chief who lived in constant fear of losing his life and property, was not joking.

The woman who brought the news was still standing at a respectable three or four meter from them.

"What did you say?" he looked up at the woman with renewed eagerness, as the muscles around his mouth formed a vicious smile.

"Achiebio will have course t o celebrate today," she repeater, rubbing her hands delightfully, as if she expected to be rewarded. Eshuo-Fuo looked at Nkem-Fuo and both smiled. Referring to the fact that the Chief had never had to celebrate, Eshuo-Fuo mused: "When a poor dancer gets the dancing steps, he does not want the dance to stop."

"What? Do I have a Chopchair or not? My ears are open. Let my ancestors hear that it was your own lips which first said it." And before the woman answered he struck his throat chest proudly:

"I always knew that there was a son somewhere in Ngwika's waist. Tell me." He held out his horn again to Nkem-Fuo who rose and poured him another drink.

"Achiebio has not only one but two Chopchairs," she announced with great excitement.

Chapter Five

This was one of those typical mid-October days when the weather was most unpredictable. One whole week of fine weather had given way to another wee of rain. Grey clouds blanketed the sky day after day. Storms of continuous thunder,-like the rolling of stones down the topless hills that surrounded Betaranda, alternated with periods of monotonous drizzle and occasional sunshine like the on they were having on that fateful day.

Fuo-Akendong's temperament was as changeable as the weather in which they were living. As if a smile had never settled on it, his brows came together to form the usual frown, transforming his forehead into chevrons. He bit his right thumbnail until a piece stuck between his teeth. He pulled it out, spat and snarled in a tone that made the woman tremble with terror: "Two how?"

"Ngwika has delivered twins. Two boys like this." With her left hand she held her clenched right fist out to him as an indication of virility. She was a stranger to the palace and so was too excited with what she considered very good news to notice the bad effect that the news of two males had on the Chief.

As if he had been openly insulted, Fuo-Akendong seized the calabash from Nkem-Fuo and flung it in the direction of the woman shattering it into smithereens. He ground his teeth, gnawed at his lower lip and began to breathe fast. Perspiration burst suddenly from his creased forehead. At the same time he pressed the mouth of the horn between his right thumb and index finger until the horn cracked, an incredible feat in itself. That was a bad sign.

***

Nkem-Fuo and Eshuo had served Fuo-Akendong for 11 years as his adviser and could read the Chief's mind like one reads a book. Nkem-Fuo took just one look at Fuo-Akendong and immediately concluded that the news of two males rather than one had struck a distinct note of anger and disappointment. The scowl which he knew to be a permanent feature on Fuo-Akendong's face deepened. His face seemed to sag. The age lines that ran like a pair of dividers from the outside of his nostrils into the comers of his mouth deepened into gorges.

The old man immediately recalled some tales he had heard narrated by Fuo-Akendong himself about the vicious nature of twins. Their tradition feared and abhorred twins. It was common knowledge that twins were ghost children. Some said that many generations ago they were thrown into the river immediately they were delivered.

A woman who delivered twins twice ran the risk of losing her life. Twins were said to bring much misery to families. From a purely economic standpoint, it was not easy to bring them up successfully. And it was universally believed that they could not be reared apart that whenever on fell sick the other was sure to follow suite. They were said to have supernatural power communicated with evil spirits and could bring such spirits along with much mishap to the families into which they were born.

Two successors, each of whom will lay a claim to the throne, Fuo-Akendong sighed. He took in a long breath and throwing the damaged horn across the lawn he gave voice to his disappointment:

"God gives you by the right and takes away by the left. I ask for a Chopchair, and instead of giving me one he gives two. So that they should fight and kill themselves over my property. Why twins, oh God? What have I done that you should punish me this way....?" He lifted his eyes and, looking at the woman he blasted: "Get out of my sight."

"But, Achiebio," Nkem-Fuo tried to persuade him" Whatever God gives, we take with two hands..."

"Enough!" the Chief shouted. "This is not the work of God. It is the work of Satan. God cannot allow you to gather your termites and then let the birds to feed on it. So shut up," he ended up, stamping his foot so loudly that the dog barked outside. "When something pains me and I am vomiting, don't hold my throat. A boil has burst in my throat, let me swallow the pus alone. One more word and nobody will ever know that you ever had a tongue in that you month. You hear?"

"Achiebio," the old man admitted and then sat back in frightened silence. The Chief rose and with his head lowered, sauntered towards his room, musing. Somewhere in the middle of the parlour he turned and came back.

"See what trouble the birth of only one child brings to a family," he spoke as if to himself. "You will think that the new child is a stranger who has come to seize their mother from the rest of the children, and even from her husband. And then you have four *njangmbins* to sit on one throne! Is that not just giving me sleepless night? I knew that Ngwika will one day remove sleep from my eyes." He smacked his lips walked away through the parlour into his room banging the door violently behind him.

Chapter Six

The two elders had several fears, genuine ones! The first was that based on what they had heard so far, Ngwika has instantly earned the Chief's hatred. The second fear was that the Chief had instantly developed a hatred for one of the boys. And everybody knew that he had a frightening way of dealing with people he hated.

Even if he had not voiced it, the two old men knew how much he cared about how his kingdom would pass to his successor. They would not be surprised to hear that one of the twins had been killed, if that was to guarantee the peaceful transition of power from him to his successor. There was something else they knew: their Chief loved flattery and so could be very easily deceived.

The bearer of the news was not a permanent resident of the palace, and so much could be made of this detail, something which could make the consequences less catastrophic. The two men conferred and then Eshuo-Fuo walked to the window and spoke from out side to the obvious hearing of the Chief.

"Achiebio," he began most persuasively. "My blood tells me that something is wrong. Let me go to Lemvoah and see for myself. You know these women how they see things and how they say them. It is not possible that God can decide to punish a man like you with two Chopchairs. I will want to see the truth and report it as it is."

***

That same day, determined to twist the truth to please Fuo-Akendong and so spare the lives of many other persons, the two old men left for Mvoa, ready to get, borrow or steal a female baby if possible in order to use for their purpose. At Mvoa, all the omens were so much in their favour that they did not need to steal or beg for a baby. As God would have it, Rosa Mbeunzoa, Ngwika's widowed elder sister, had just given birth to a baby girl in the same health centre.

They communicated the emotions of the Chief to the two women and the hospital attendants and then Nkem-Fuo made a proposal to Rosa who lost her husband three months into her pregnancy and convinced her to switch babies. They were sisters, it was argued, and were forced to do so just to please the Chief and save the life of one of the children. He assured the women that if the two boys entered the palace the Chief would not be pleased until one of them had died.

The two mothers saw some sense in what the men suggested. Nkwika was especially gratified because she knew how easily her husband could act out his anger. Rosa who had lost four children all in infancy, was relieved that somebody else would have to take care of her baby, just in case the death of the others resulted from her way of bringing them up. The persons it took a longer time to persuade were the mid-wife and two nurses. The midwife understood their predicament and sympathised with them. But she asked:

"And now that the Chief already knows that you delivered two boys, how will we be able to convince him about this new idea?"

"Leave that to us," Nkem-Fuo told her. "We are the Chief's ears, we are his mouth. We will tell him what he wants to hear." He then turned to the nurse and pleaded:

22

"My daughter, do us only one favour. Let the world of no other version of the story than that Nkwika delivered a boy and a girl, and that her sister delivered a boy. Let us five swear to die with this secret. If we keep out mouths shut, the discovery will not be made in our life time. Nor in the Chief's."

***

Armed with this information Nkem-Fuo returned with his friend late that evening to the palace in Betaranda. It was one of those many moments when the Chief was in no mood to receive anybody because he was just about to have his supper, which looked like a meal for ten men! One of his wives had prepared two large bundles of *egusi* pudding and ten fingers of plantains to go with. In a small leaf she had also tied a handful of palm tree maggots. The second had prepared *Abe-Nchi*, a large bowl of pounded *coco yams* and fried pumpkin leaves. A third had prepared *fufu*-corn and a bowl of dried tadpoles and two large crabs to go with. There was also a big bowl of pepper soup made from the intestines of a pig, and assortment of fruits and half a bunch of bananas.

In a small bag in the centre of the table stood a bottle of drink. It could not have been WHISKY BLACK, so the two old men guessed that it must be red wine, most probably the popular CASANOVA (which the Chief himself called Cassava). It was the one drink he could be easily caught drinking alone, whenever he was eating.

When the two men arrived at the door and noticed that heed was about to go to table they hesitated for a long time before announcing their presence. And they even decided to announce their presence simply because they knew the Chief would be glad to listen to them. When the last woman placed her basket on the table he ordered her out and then shut the door. He then went into his room and dug from under his bed two small cubes in a small parcel. They turned out to be HONK CUBES which he himself called HONEY KING always kept to spice his meals a after his wives had served him and gone.

The two old men greeted from outside. Something in the Chief told him that the people must be bringing good news because he hated the bearer of bad news. And they knew that. When they and were told to come in the Chief had just peeled the paper from the small tasty cube and was using the back of his spoon to grind one of them to powder. He showed the two where to sit and continued with his ritual. He sprinkled a large quantity of the powder into the tadpole soup and a little on the pumpkin leaves, half of which he gave to the visitors.

When I have my medicine like this, he said holding up one of the cubes, "I don't care whether a women is urinating in her pot of soup."

The two men were forced to laugh with him, eyeing each other. He cut half of the *Abe-Nchi* and put in his plate and then asked Nkem-Fuo to take the rest for themselves.

""Eat before you open your mouths," the Chief said. "let me eat first," he said. "Some kind of news cannot lie quiet in an empty stomach."

"We thank Achiebio," the old men said. Half way through the meal as soon as he had served himself two cups of wine and returned the bottle to his room, the Chief could not withstand the suspense he himself had created.

"Tell me what you have found out," he shouted.

"As I suspected, Achiebio," Eshuo-Fuo began, cleaning his mouth with the back of his hand, "something in my blood shook me. That woman had reported the way women see and report things-upside down. I have a suspicious that one of those your enemies sent her to come and break your heart so that you die and leave the kingdom in their hands."

Fuo-Akendong who suspected everybody too in a long breath and looked on incredulously.

"What are you telling me?" he enquired.

"Minka who brought that news does not know the difference between Nkeika and Rosa," Nkem-Fuo stepped in. "she sees Rosa's boy and declares that he is Ngwika's. so if a person's sister delivers a child and somebody holds the child to admire the baby, that child is automatically the admirer's child?"

"Nkem," he continued. "You remember that I toll you that woman just wanted to break the Chief's heart? What will a woman gain if she causes her husband to die?"

Fuo-Akendong who was beginning to be interested in this new version of the story, blinked his eyes several times.

"You can say that because you do not know women," he said to Eshuo-Fuo."

"Get that witch Minka for me, he shouted. Having been brainwashed by Nkem-Fuo and Eshuo-Fuo, the poor woman had to retract everything that she had said.

"How many children did Nkwika deliver?" Fuo-Akendong asked severely.

"They told me that she delivered twins," she answered.

"Did you see them?" he asked.

She shook her head in denial.

Nkem – Fuo threw his hands open. "Did we not say we thought that she was lying?" he looked at the Chief. Fuo-Akendong rose, seized her right hand and twisting it behind her kicked her bottom and pushed her away.

"If next time somebody sends you to come and break my heart tell him that mine is a heart of stone." He then returned to his seat.

"Nkem," he called. "I want to believe that it is your own version of the story that is true, just because you have always been true to me, and also because you have never joined anybody who plotted to make a fool of me. But I will go to Lemvoah myself tomorrow morning to make sure."

"I will be lying to the Chief to gain what?" Nkem-Fuo asked. "The road to Lemvoah is open. I can even go there with Achiebio this very night, if that will make him sleep soundly."

Fuo-Akendong told himself that he would only believe if he went there and saw for himself. But he thought this was good reason to celebrate. He rose and entered his room himself. After a few minutes he returned cloth. It looked like some fetish. He stuck the bottle under his left armpit and used his hardened right thumb nail to open it. He took a long sip from the bottle, struck his chest and said "the man who made this thing knows what to do."

"What is it, Achiebio?" the old man asked with great curiosity.

The Chief held the cork in his right hand and poured about five drops of secret drink into it. He then held the cork of drink to Nkem-Fuo. The man took it gratefully and threw the drink into his mouth, swallowed it and then smiled.

"What is it, Achiebio?" he asked again, licking the inside of the cork.

The Chief did not answer. He took back the cork and doled out a few more drops which he gave to the old man. The man took and swallowed again in one gulp and licked the inside of the cork again.

"What does it taste like?"

"It is a great drink, quite all right," he admitted.

The Chief disclosed the contents of the black cloth: a large bottle of WHISKY BLACK which he placed on the footrest in front of him.

"When you see me with this bottle," he beamed, "know that happiness is in my heart."

He immediately recorked the bottle and put it back in the black cloth. As he rose to return to the room NKem-Fuo said almost to himself:

"Tell me how a man cannot do wonders if this is the kind of drink he takes!"

Back to the veranda he repeated that he would go to Lemvoah to make assurance double sure.

Chapter Seven

The trip to Lemvoah was not a waste of time. Fuo-Akendong saw with his own eyes a pair of twins suckling from the breasts of Ngwika, his personal wife. There was one boy and one girl, just as he had been reliably informed. There was also another baby, a boy, suckling from the breasts of Rosa, the sister of his wife, Ngwika. This too was just as he had been informed. He congratulated the two women and then left. He did not need any further proof. The source of the error was thus explained to him.

"What names have you given them?" the Chief teased them.

"Achiebio," the midwife began in the same light-hearted manner, "one person will drink and a different person will fall in the gutter? It is for you to name them"

The Chief gave them names. He called the boy his "Chopchair," but as the tradition of twins demanded, he called him Nchonganyi. He called the girl Ngenyi, the female counterpart of a male twin. He reached into his bag and took out a small parcel which he gave to Ngwika.

"Give two to your sister," he said. After he had left the women opened the parcel. It contained six pieces of the soap every respectable woman used for her laundry it was SAVON PROMO!

***

The other boy in Rosa's charge was called simply Peter. After the Chief left he was given another name, Nnwolefeck. The nursing mothers, Nkem-Fuo and Eshuo-Fffuo and the midwife chose Rosa's new abode very carefully. Because of the secret surrounding Peter Nwolefec's birth which they promised to protect, Rosa was to stay in Efong, her late husband's compound, for a few days. The new lodging agreed on was Bellua, the home of Rosa's maternal grandmother. There she lived virtually alone with her baby.

The house in which they lived was not much different from a hut: a dome-like structure of compactly arched Indian bamboos. It was covered externally by a thick layer of thatch, and rested upon a floor. It was about four meters or in diameter, of hard, dry and smoothly beaten earth. Behind this hut was a large uncompleted building of sun-dried bricks, evidence that death had taken its previous owner unawares, in the middle of a major project. The building had four bedrooms, two on either side of large parlour. Part of the roof covering up to half the parlour had been roofed with zinc. The rest was bare with only decaying rafters and purlins.

Here they lived for four years. Rosa did not engage the services of a baby-sitter. Again that was because she did not want the secret about peter Nwolefeck to be known. During the early months and much into the first year she mostly farmed around the house, leaving him in bed. A very active child from birth, he rolled and fell once. Thereafter she decided to place him on a mat on the floor while she worked. On market days she would fasten him on her back and carry her vegetables, fruits and plantains or other food items in a basket on her head.

Part Two

You need not tell all the truth, unless to those who have a right to know it all. But let all you tell be the truth
(HORACE MANN)

Chapter Eight

Peter Nwolefeck developed very fast, do fast that by the fifteenth month he could walk. This made life a lot easier for Rosa who could them take him along with her to her more distant farms. She would allow him to sit and play in the furrows while she did her planting. Some times he sat on leaves on a shade of palm fronts and plantain leaves while she weeded or harvested. All along even though she got a pair of ear-rings which she stuck to his eats and continued to wear him girls clothes, nobody else but herself knew that Peter Nwolefeck was a boy and not a girl. Once in a while Ngwika would visit them, bringing gifts.

***

The burden which Rosa, Nkem-Fuo and the Mvoa Health Centre attendants had taken on themselves was not as easy as they thought. It was easy to convince the Chief about what he was seeing and turn him back happily. But for how long were they to keep such a secret. So long as the Chief lived the truth was bound to filter in to his ears one day.

The traditional Lebang/Lewoh animosity was intensifying everyday. Most of the attendants at Mvoa were from Lebang and so the Lewoh women could not trust them to keep their secret for too long. The possibility was always there, that if only to embarrass Lewoh, those attendants could let the cat out of the bag at any moment.

"When Nkem-Fuo and his friend were persuading the midwife to co-operate with them, one of the attendants was overheard saying;" they are Lewohs. If they want to throw their babies into a pit latrine, let them go right ahead. After all, what has a rat got to do with a bottle?"

A more serious source of worry was the child from whom it could not be kept forever. They had not considered all possibilities. The decisions they took at that moment were short-sighted. Ngwika would visit Rosa and her son as often as possible and offer any kind of assistance they would need. Rosa would also visit her daughter in the palace whenever she wanted. Ngwika would manage to obtain money from the Chief and give to the boy to settle on his own in Kumba or anywhere else in the Coast. When he was big enough to know things, they would tell him the favour they did to him, how they had saved his life and theirs. It never occurred to them that he would do anything else but express gratitude to them.

What the Chief saw when he came to the hospital was mere make-belief. Problems started right at the Health Centre. The boy would not suckle Rosa's breast, neither would Rosa's daughter suckle Ngwika's breasts. When in the end the infants were forced to accept the breast milk from the women, the two women could not give them enough motherly care/ the thought that her own child was being nurse by some other person far away in the palace disturbed Rosa. It did not matter that the girl was in very good hands. She wanted to take part on her child's development, especially because she was the one thing that reminded her of her late husband.

This lack of love affected Peter Nwolefeck's state of mind as he grew up. It was as if he were an orphan. This, coupled with the fiery behaviour he inherited from his father made him a very strange being.

In fact, so strong was this feeling that at one time when Ngwika visited them and the boy's fate was the subject of conversation, Rosa told her to take the boy away and damn the consequences. She told Ngwika that she had run out of lies, and Peter Nwolefect asked far too many questions which she was unable to answer sincerely and satisfactorily.

***

He was very fast learner, but even at the tender age of four, he had one unmanageable problem: his temper. Rosa reared fowls but was not bold enough to cut the throat of a chicken. Peter Nwolefeck gave notice of what king of person he would be in future by either wringing the neck of the chicken or cutting the throat by placing his left foot on the wings and the legs and stretching out the neck before cutting it.

One day when he killed a cock and Rosa gave him the head, feet and intestines, which was what they used to eat as children, peter Nwolefeck flung the whole bowl of soup into the fire.

"Who will eat the breast and the legs?" he asked furiously.

"If your father were here he would eat it," the woman said.

"But now that he is not here, I have to eat it, because I am a man because I killed the fowl myself," he said.

Chapter Nine

The way the young boy reacted to petty injustices made Rosa very uncomfortable. The more so because nobody knew the truth about his life better than herself. She refrained from discussing anything about his father, under the pretext that his death hurt her so much that she did not like talking about it to him. Ever so often he would ask to know why she had decided that he should be dressed like a girl. On each occasion she gave a different answer, that when he was delivered the only clothes she had around were girls' clothes; that she had wanted only a girl and that dressing him in that manner satisfied that inner wish.

Sometimes she would forget completely that Peter Nwolefeck was not a girl. She would undress in front of him before realising it and turning to look at the gaping eyes of the little boy. One day when she took off her dress in front of him the little asked in all innocence:" When I grow up will I also be like that?" he was referring to her curious anatomy which differed so much from his.

"You will be even taller than me," she replied diverting attention from the main issue.

When the searching questions persisted, Rosa thought it was time to move away so that Peter Nwolefeck should assume his true nature as a boy. If he was then going to dress like a boy that would have to happen far away from Belua. Not that too many people visited them, but she could never tell who would betray them. Ngwika and herself agreed that she should move with Peter Nwolefeck to Nzenawung. There they were to live in the compound of a deceased relative.

The inquisitive Peter Nwolefeck never stopped asking why he had been dressed like a girl from the start. None of the answers which were given seemed to satisfy him. One day, Rosa decided to tell him the truth, or at least part of the truth:

"I decided to dress you up as a girl in order to solve a very complicated problem," she said. "When you are 14 years old I will tell you the whole truth," she announced. She was thinking particularly of an age at which he could be easily apprenticed to a trade rather than one at which he could reason with them.

Peter Nwolefeck would have to wait for seven years. During that time Rosa and Ngwika naively hopes that the Chief would die and so make the revelation easy for everybody. They too would wait a long time because there were no signs that the Chief would die soon.

***

About three kilometres away from Nzenawung, there lived Pa Ambrose (called by the native Amblushi). He was the village catechist and the closest thing to a Priest. In the absence of a priest people went to him for confession. Peter Nwolefeck's fate was becoming more and more disturbing to Rosa. It was to Ambrose that she went one day and confessed her part in the crime she committed with her sister. She told the man the whole truth and then pleaded with him to come to her house and help her explain the problem to the boy and ask for forgiveness.

"It is you to do it," the catechist insisted. "If somebody else does, it will not have the desired effect. You have to talk to him yourself and make him see that you did it out of love for him.

Peter Nwolefect was just thirteen then, but there was something intensely scaring about him. She was unsure as to how he would react to the truth. As she travelled back

36

home an idea struck her. She would tell the story to Peter Nwolefeck as if she heard it from somebody else and about somebody else. That way, she would even prepare his mind for the eventual revelation.

***

When she got home and told the story, Peter's smouldering anger seemed to burst into flames. He would not even let her finish the story.

"If I was the one who was disinherited like that," he warned, "I would burn down that palace. Through no fault of his a child is sent away from the palace to live in poverty just to please a wicked Chief! If I was the one I would kill them all."

Rosa was paralysed with stupefaction. As if that was not enough, Peter Nwolefeck kept track of every day and month that passed. On his fifteenth birthday he came up to his mother and asked for the truth she had been hiding. Rosa visited Ngwika and the two agreed that he should know the truth. Ngwika made the sum of 50,000francs available to the sister which would be used to pay for the learning of some trade.

On her way back her imagination got the better of her. He wishes too control of her mind and she immediately saw in he mind's eye not what could happen but what she would like to see happen. She saw herself telling the whole story to the boy. She saw the youth jump up and embrace her. She heard him say: "Mother, when you told me the story the other day I was annoyed because I did not think that such a thing could happen. After that I thought for myself and saw that a woman who does that to a child really loves the child. I am glad that I am still alive and I am grateful that you did all that just to save me. So I shall never do anything to make you suffer for saving me…."

That same night that she returned she decided to tell the boy the truth.

"The story I told you one day which you hated to hear so much, my son, was your own story," she began. "Your are that prince who was disinherited." She went on to tell him the whole truth, including the fact that the woman who came to see them often with gifts was indeed his mother. To appease him further, she immediately showed him the money that had been given for him and ask him to choose some trade.

***

What happened next frightened he. Peter did none of the things she had imagined he would do. He remained calm throughout the recital, and even found it amusing. When she finished talking he rose, smacked his lips and gnawing at his lower lip smiled dryly as he walked away.

For some reason he thought she was simply teasing him. His very first reaction was to doubt the veracity of the story. The story weighed on him like a log of wood. Two days later, to reassure himself, he asked her to repeat the story. After telling him again she noticed a disturbing silence and gloom about Peter Nwolefeck.

"So what do you plan to do?" she asked.

"Just wait, mami," he responded.

"What kind of trade would you like to choose?" she asked.

"Just wait, mami," he said.

She said nothing more, but she knew that the issue was far from over.

Chapter Ten

Not many families or villages in the Lebialem Division at the time were lucky to have schools located on their neighbourhood. The lucky few sent their children there at ages as young as six. Quite often school was a very long distance away, in some cases as far as five kilometres from most homes. Pupils had to cross extremely difficult terrain to steep hills and deep valleys to get there. If you sipped and fell, there was very little chance of surviving because you would break many bones on your body by the time you reached the bottom of the hill where your body would finally settle.

Consequently, it was not surprising that children in class one were as old as fourteen. They needed to be strong enough to protect and defend themselves before venturing out of their homes for the hazardous journey to school. In a majority of cases, when the terrain was not much of a threat, more discouraging obstacles awaited them in the schools themselves. There, because of their ages and sizes, the big bullies were the laughing stock of much younger and brighter pupils who answered all the questions, and who lived near the schools. This made the big boys very uneasy and unenthusiastic about school.

Where the big boys were not the butt of jokes from smaller ones, they were the victims of a brutal system. In those days school was associated with punishment and torture rather than education. The story was told that between the age of six and twelve, Fuo-Akendong refused to send his "Chopchair" to school, for fear that he would be beaten by teachers. The story goes that during that period he sent a relative living with him to study and report back everyday to his son what the teacher had taught them after beating them. The slave did so for six years, passing only four examinations. Then one day somebody told the Chief that if the boy did well and a scholarship came for somebody to be sent to college, it was the boy and not his Chopchair that would benefit. Only then did he decide to send his Chopchair to school.

That changed the spirit of the people of Betaranda towards education somewhat. Somewhat, because many of those who had the opportunities to go to school were not much better off. There was the perennial absence of seasoned teachers. So-called "sons and daughters of the soil" who had acquired professional training down the coast, and whose presence would have alleviated the problem, refused to work in their own villages. Outsiders were reluctant to render services there since it was clear that the natives themselves hated the place. Many of the teachers were themselves dull, poorly trained employees of the PARENTS-TEACHERS ASSOCIATIONS. In many cases they had been permitted to complete their courses in the Government Teachers Training College mainly because they sponsored their education there rather than that they had exhibited any particular ability either intellectually or professionally.

The upshot or all this was that youths found farming, fishing or hunting around the villages a more profitable and less embarrassing occupation. They eventually gave up the idea of school altogether.

This was precisely the situation that confronted Peter Nwolefeck. His was confounded, however, by the fact that they needed to keep him in hiding.

***

In the neighbourhood were his peers, vagabonds, hunters, thieves, fishermen. They called themselves *"Bambe*s", which simply meant the desperate ones. They were generally seen in groups of fours and fives. For some reason they always added an S to name. In Peter Nwolefeck's group which he virtually led there were seven *Bambe*s: *Bambe* Peters himself, *Bambe* Isaiahs, *Bambe* Sams, *Bambe*Nchongs, *Bambe* Mantros,*Bambe* Caps and *Bambe* Cos.

After Rosa convinced him by telling him the story of his life for the second time, *Bambe* Peters immediately summoned his *Bambe*s to whom he related the story. It was too good to be true. At first none of the other *Bambe*s seemed to believe. What made them pay attention was just the fact that he was a boy of very serious disposition. And when it became obvious that he was speaking the truth, they all began to find out how they could turn the whole matter into their advantage.

At the end of the story, *Bambe* Peters stand was clear: there would be no such thing as going to the Coast! He needed his own share of the inheritance, and the *Bambe*s must do everything within their reach to ensure that he got it. At the back of his mind, he had decided that if the worst came to the worst, he would keep the Chopchair hostage, compel the Chief to give enough money for him to go down to the Coast and set up a business.

He would ask that his own share of the inheritance be converted to cash or to land he could sell. But then it soon became evident that if he worked hard he could actually become the Chief. If they killed the Chief and Chopchair, the throne was securely his. So why worry?

"Instead of asking for the leg of the cow, why not take the whole cow and then cut the part we need? Why only part of the inheritance?" one of them asked. "What stops you from taking the whole kingdom and being Chief?"

The likelihood of having one of their kinds in the chair of rule drove them all to frenzy. They saw *Bambe*s taking over the world. They would kill the twin rival, kill Fuo and put *Bambe* Peters on the throne. With *Bambe* Peters on the throne they who helped him to power would be rewarded with positions of eminence in the palace, as well as land for farming, grazing or selling. All his advisers would be *Bambe*s. They would collect taxes and beat up people who did not co-operate. If a *Bambe* climbs plums, they all thought, the black ones must go only to the *Bambe*s! They saw their long suffering finally at an end.

Chapter Eleven

ambe Peters welcomed the ideas and was happy with their determination to give him back his due, or at least recover what he had lost. But he cautioned them: "Although we want that throne very badly, I want us to think about what we are going to do before we start. We should not put our feet into hot waters. What if the story my mother has told me is not true? If even it is true, and there was another prince in the palace like myself, is it going to be easy for us to march into the palace of a dangerous Chief and seize power? If that Chief is indeed my father, then I do not think that…"

"That man whom I hear is like a tiger, if his sons are like *Bambe* Peters," one of them chipped in, pointing at Peter Nwolefeck, "then the two of them, plus the other males in the compound can combine to peel the skin off our backs."

They all therefore resolved to give the entire endeavour a second thought.

***

When the issue was referred back to *Bambe* peters he told them:

'To succeed we have to know many things, very many things. First I want to know whether…"

He pulled up his *jumpa* and revealed a tattoo with a curious design above the navel. "I want to know whether there is somebody in the palace who has this same thing. He told them what his mother had told him when revealing his past to him: that whenever twins are delivered each is given an identical mark on an identical spot, a different one for a girl.

"We have to establish," he continued, "that there is someone, sixteen years old who looks exactly like me in the palace. I want a *Bambe* to go to the palace or to the school or wherever. We will also have to establish that there was a girl of my age who was born on the same day with me and who has not this mark, but a circle.'

The venture offered so much excitement that volunteers were not lacking. He had hardly finished talking when *Bambe* Isaiahs volunteered to spy on the prince. His offer was quickly accepted because the mission involved going to the school compound. Amongst them all, he was the only one to have set foot in a school compound.

***

Bambe Isaiahs' strategy bore all the hallmarks of genius! First his investigations established that the Prince attended Government School at 4-Cormers Foto. He arrived the G.S. compound early the next day and took up a sitting position from which he could see all those who came up from Betaranda or the Nkwini-Nkeh hills. He had no problem recognising his foe, who looked so much like *Bambe* Peters that had it not been for his neat dress he would have easily mistaken the prince for *Bambe* Peters. The striking resemblance spurred him to pursue the rest of the investigation because it now meant that with just a little effort a *Bambe* would be Chief, with the others occupying positions of honour in a place previously reserved for a chosen few.

As we the case n many of the schools in the Division, there were very few teachers, and so he was not afraid of being apprehended. In fact, in this particular school, there

44

were only two teachers, the Headmaster and a lady whom they called Miss. He hung around the school until it was break time and them he accosted the prince to whom he introduced himself as a prince of the royal line of Small Monje, seeking admission into school.

He said (and which was true!) that he had attended school up to class 4 in their village but wanted to change. He bought groundnuts and bananas which the two of them ate. He said he would study the place, teachers, pupils and even the weather before making up his mind about transferring.

He resurfaced immediately after school and continuing his conversation, he indicated that he would need a sleeping place for that evening before returning to Small Monje to make up his mind. There in the school the Prince was considered extremely proud. Additionally, his wealthy background alienated him from the other children, so that he did not have any real friends. It was not that he was unfriendly. Just that the other children felt themselves too inferior to enjoy his company.

He was therefore surprisingly pleased to find somebody talk to him so freely, somebody, above all, of royal blood. He did not object to the noble stranger's request to spend the night in the palace. The Prince introduced *Bambe* to his father just as the stranger had introduced himself. He was well received and he spent a good night in the palace. *Bambe* hardly slept for he needed to know everything about the palace – where the Prince slept, where he bathed, how his father treated him and vice-versa – before leaving the next day. And he was able to take much along with him.

Chapter Twelve

The following day, on the pretext that he was going back to Small Monje to think over what to do, *Bambe* Isaiahs returned to Nzenawung and reported his findings. There was not only a male counterpart but an identical twin of the same height, complexion, size, with the same tell-tale mark, and that there was such a girl as he wanted to know.

That afternoon Peter Nwolefect told Rosa:

"If you want to know what I want to do with the story you told me, listen but do not stop me."

The woman sat down and listened with eyes already clouding with tears.

"I am going back to the palace to claim my own share of the kingdom...."

"But the Chief has not yet divided the kingdom. He has not given anything to your brother..."

"Then I will go there and enjoy as he has done all these years."

"Listen to me, my son," she pleaded, "that man you call your father , you do not know him. He will kill you. He will kill all of us."

"He won't," Peter Nwolefect sad firmly, cocksurely.

"My son," she implored him further. "Have I not showed you the money which my sister, your mother and myself have agreed which you will go down to the Coast and use to learn a trade?"

Peter Nwolefeck had started shaking his head in refusal long before she finished talking. As soon as she stopped speaking she looked across at him.

"My mother," he said softly. "You do not understand…"

"It is you who so not understand," she cut in. "Your father is a brute. What ever we have done has been to save you, to save my life, to save your mother…"

"But you have not saved me. You have simply killed me… look at me. I spend six years behaving like a girl. That means I have missed learning the things boys are supposed to don for the first six years in my life. And you say you were saving me? I haven't gone to school. I know no book. I cannot write my name, I cannot read a letter… I have not learned anything. Nothing. And you say you were saving me?"

The woman held her head in her hands and wept bitterly. Peter Nwolefeck had unwittingly made many telling points. As far as learning a trade was concerned, he had lost very much. It is true that Rosa allotted to him a small garden-plot which she insisted he should tend himself to furnish foodstuff for the house. It is true that she caused him to sweep the house and surrounding yard, fetch water in gourds from neighbouring springs or streams, sometimes boil maize and prepare other foods for the approaching meal. But this was very little compared to what happened to the children in the palace.

Apart from Chopchair, there were many other males in the palace – nephews and simple hangers-on. Although Fuo Akendong detested any son who was not his since becoming Chief, he took care of them, nevertheless. While preserving the secrets of his magical powers for his Chopchair, he made it a point of duty to apprentice each of the male children to some kind of trade: a manufacturing of ornaments or medicinal herbs; doctoring, divining, metal work, wood-carving, basket-making, stock-castrating and the like.

All Peter Nwolefect knew he was good for were, therefore, the menial skills: erecting new and various fences around the compound, hewing down the bush and cutting long grass from such spots as his aunt would want to

48

cultivate, paring new sticks. He knew nothing about going to school, or to church and little about God in fact, the only occasion he usually heard about God was when Rosa insulted him after he had committed a mischief.

"God will punish you one day for all these things that you are doing to me," she would say.

Chapter Thirteen

"**A**re you sure saying that we should have allowed you to be killed?" Rosa queried.

"I did not say I wanted to be killed. The question I am asking is 'But why me?' if we were twins, why should I have been the one to suffer?"

"It could have gone either way," she said.

"But it went the wrong way, coming to me," he said unyieldingly.

The woman knelt down in front of the boy and discharged a flood of tear, reflected for a while and pleaded further:

"Peter Nwolefeck, my child, I am begging you. Before you embark on anything, give me time to talk to your mother, my sister."

"When are you talking to her?"

"Next market day," she said.

It was Peter Nwolefeck's turn to reflect. After a whole minutes he told her:" do not talk to my mother. I will tell you when to talk to her."

***

Peter Nwolefeck's suggestion that Rosa should not talk to his mother was simply to gain time. That same evening he reassembled his friends and released the information to them. He then revealed the next plan of action.

"Since this boy whom *Bambe* says they call Chopchair looks exactly like me, I want us to devise a means of capturing him and keeping him away while I sit in the palace."

There was first a slight relief and then an atmosphere of unease and disappointed seemed to set in. The lot of them thought he was about to let slip the one opportunity to make their lives better. This feeling was not unjustified. When the thought first crossed his mind he contemplated killing Chopchair outright and remaining sole prince. He had even ventured to voice this idea to one of them! Upon second thought, it occurred to him that such an act might provoke much more serious problems. His mother and aunt would not be spared. They may even be the first to betray him or plot his own death. He therefore settled on kidnapping.

***

Bambe Peters commanded a lot of respected amongst his peers, so much so that whenever he said something, he was very rarely contradicted. They all therefore bought the idea of kidnapping the Chopchair and putting Peter in his place. Even though they were mere teenagers, they worked out the plans for the kidnapping as if they were a team of mercenaries hired to topple a tyrannical regime. It was unanimously agreed that since *Bambe* Isaiahs had already made himself a friend to the prince, he was to lead the mission.

The plans to kidnap the Prince and put *Bambe* Peters in his place took exactly seven days to be realized. During this time, Peter Nwolefeck reassured Rosa that he had changed his mind about going to the palace. He settle in the Coast or choosing a particular kind of trade for a while before giving his final reply. Because she was anxious to please him and so avoid any further distress, she did not resist his proposition.

As part of the plan to bring him closer to their target, *Bambe* Isaiahs returned the day after the decision was made to tell the prince that he had finally decided to enrol in G.S.

4-Corners Foto. On this particular trip he learned many more things: he got the colours and the sizes of the prince's sandals in the process. But, by far the most important discovery was that although the prince and *Bambe* Peters looked exactly alike, the prince was not as strong, not as brilliant and not as daring as *Bambe* Peters.

Bambe Isaiahs even declared: "I can tie up the pig with only one hand and carry away." This automatically implied that the kidnapping would pose no physical danger. It would have been harder for them if they had to deal with *Bambe* Peters instead.

Chapter Fourteen

To avoid drawing suspicion on themselves, they decided to enact the act of kidnapping Chopchair and taking him home several times before the day. First on Monday, and then on Wednesday, at the Alou market square, all seven of them (who were quite known as jobless rascals) suddenly seized and surrounded *Bambe* Peters, tied his hands behind his back and marched him down the road into the bush towards Nzenawung where they planned to imprison Chopchair. Passers-by who were at first worried soon got used to what they began to describe as "the young men's dry season madness."

And then on Monday the following week the pot was hatched. The kidnapping proper drew less suspicion than the first two rehearsals. Immediately school closed *Bambe* Isaiahs simply invited Chopchair to show him the new compound in which he would be living. As soon as they were a good distance into where the *Bambe*s were hiding, they jumped from the bush and seized him as practised.

The place where the captive was to be taken and hidden was an abandoned compound behind a hill and across a small stream that flowed under gigantic rocks through which erosion and time, like some superhuman artist, had carved and swept away the inside of a large cave, leaving but a huge archway. You passed through the archway and across the stream into a clearing where women and men from their farms placed the items, rested and took a bath before proceeding to their homes. Rising immediately behind the clearing was another hill.

It was from a vantage point behind this hill that *Bambe* Peters was to view the action. Without being seen himself he could see everybody passing through the archway, crossing the stream and resting in the clearing. The story went that in the good old days during inter-tribal wars, many an enemy was trapped and slaughtered from the same position. As he sat in this hideout *Bambe* Peters told himself that if the captive turned out to be much different from himself, he would let him go because it would be suicide to attempt to substitute somebody he did not resemble.

***

What he saw baffled him. A youth of about his own height and complexion was being led through the archway across the stream into the clearing. His hands were tied behind him. He took out the small mirror he had carried in his pocket and looked from it to the stranger, to cross-check the resemblance. He looked at it, at first casually, and them when the likeness became increasingly strong he looked into it much more carefully. He even pulled at his own jaws and touched his lips to make sure that they were the same as those he was beholding.

The apparent difference between his face and that of the stranger was that the stranger looked fresher. *Bambe* Peters' features were a bit harsher, due to the nature of his upbringing. The stranger, on his part, had had luxury and attention ever since he was born, especially during the days when somebody else went to school and received punishment on his behalf. His hands, like *Bambe* Peters', were large but supple with almost whitish palms. Like *Bambe* Peters he had a large skull with thick hair that grew to just above his eyebrows, giving him a severe look. In the end *Bambe* Peters was persuaded that every bit of information he had received was correct. This was, in fact, his double.

And this realization strengthened his belief in what he had decided to do. There was more than envy, jealousy and admiration when *Bambe* Peters'. For one thing, there was nothing of the icy hardness, nothing of the scowl, the morbid melancholy that was permanently stamped on *Bambe* Peters' visage. He had the same wide expressive thickly lashed eyes.

His jaws were not chiselled like *Bambe* Peters' but round and fleshy. He looked like on who must have had more than his fair share of spoiling: very well cared for, he was wearing a very new and well-ironed sky blue shirt over an equally well-ironed khaki pair of shorts which was the Government school uniform. Whereas most the children either went on bare feet on torn shoes for above his ankle, over thick expensive-looked socks.

Chapter Fifteen

When he was led into the centre of the clearing the prisoner's hands were untied but he remained surrounded by the bands of shabbily dressed rascals. They were all dressed in patched, dirty shorts which were actually trousers that had been trimmed. Two of them wore singlettes and battered hats made from cane.

Up to this moment nobody had told him what was going on. Each time he tried to know what he had done one of them would simply say: "Just come, you will see."

While he stood looking round the band of pranksters like an antelope surrounded by a park of hounds, he heard a movement from behind the hill. Then *Bambe* Peters appeared, having already got over the shock of discovering somebody exactly like himself.

Ngwika had never mentioned the fact to him, and so the discovery caused the Chopchair greater chagrin. While they led him into the clearing, he saw himself in a dream land. Once or twice he asked his kidnappers whether it was a dream he was living through of a reality. His face-to-face confrontation with *Bambe* Peters converted the dream into a nightmare.

When *Bambe* Peters descended into the clearing they showed Chopchair a high rock on which to sit and ringed him on both sides. As *Bambe* Peters moved towards him Chopchair rubbed his eyes first with the left and then with the right hand. Though the prisoner looked lost, *Bambe* Peters was in complete control of himself. God had delivered his enemy into his hands. Here was the being, he thought with murderous envy and hate, whose existence had caused him to be driven from the palace to live like a pauper. The man whose would make him the heir and even chief of Betaranda! The thought of it darkened his face like the coming of night over a blue sky and everything about Chopchair suddenly offended *Bambe* Peters.

"It is because of you that I am suffering here," *Bambe* Peters said to him.

Chopchair felt his heart five a little jerk. "I don't understand what you mean," he said in panic.

"You are wondering who it is before you now looking exactly like you."

There was a silence.

"Am I right?" *Bambe* Peters asked.

"You are," Chopchair stammered.

"Did your mother never tell you that she delivered twins?"

'She told me. The other girl in the palace…"

"The only other twin is a boy, he is me, Peter Nwolefeck," he said striking his chest in an unforgiving tone

"*Bambe* Peters pulled down his own pair of trousers and pointed to his own birth mark.

"Does this mean anything to you?" he enquired pulling his trousers back up an tying it up with a rope.

A horrible fear had now spring to life within Chopchair. He stared at the mark for a long time and then nodding his head said: "It does."

For how long have you been in the palace?" *Bambe* Peters asked.

"Since I was born," he said trembling.

"Are you not 16 years old?"

"I am."

Bambe Peters stared at his prisoner with malevolent eyes for a long time and then asked:

"Do you know what is going to happen to you now?"

With perspiration running down his trembling cheeks, his heart hammering as it had never done before in his short life, he answered:

"No, sa."

It was not that he thought *Bambe* Peters was an adult. It was simply that what he was going through was akin to the torture he usually received from his teachers who were known by no other title but "sa."

"I am going back to the palace to continue to do the things that you were doing there," *Bambe* Peter resumed. "You will remain here…"

"Doing what?" Chopchair enquired.

"Doing the things *Bambe* has been doing all these years," *Bambe* Sams cut it.

"For how long?" Chopchair asked.

"Until he comes back," *Bambe* Mantros told him.

"For as long as you were in the palace,' *Bambe* Cos put in with the kind of contempt and envy that the poor usually have for the rich in difficulty.

Chapter Sixteen

Already thinking of himself in the position of a Chief, *Bambe* Peters whispered something to *Bambe* Cos. With his scattered teeth and shoeless feet and, trembling like a man in the grip of a fever be immediately rose and went and stood in front of Chochair.

We are going to ask you several questions," he began with an offensive pride that was cut through with a death threat. "if you answer correctly and honestly, we will do nothing to you. We have suffered too much on this earth. This is out only chance. But if try to tell a lie," he sighed and bit his right fore finger.

Someone was heard sharpening a cutlass.

"What is that?" Chopchair asked vainly trying to turn his head in the direction of the sound. "Have you not said that you will not do anything bad to me?"

Bambe Cos smiled as he walked away from their prisoner. "You have not even seen anything yet," he said.

"We only want you to know that we shall do something to you if you try to fool us."

"I cannot fool you, Sa," Chopchair swore.

There was a very long silence during which *Bambe* Peters confided with *Bambe* Cos once more. *Bambe* Cos walked up to Chopchair and asked him several questions: whether he fell sick, approximately how many times a day, a week, a month etc; what he usually suffered from —head ache, catarrh, cough, filarial and the like.

Chopchair responded as best he could. He had been sick of head ache several years ago. At which *Bambe* Cos asked:

"With all that comfort, how can you be sick? For us we sleep with diseases everyday and night."

Chopchair did not answer him. He merely enquired:

"If you are going to the palace now and leaving me like this, what have I done? Do you think it was my fault that you were sent here?"

There was no response.

"When I was in the palace, was my brother tied like this?" he asked.

Bambe Peters smiled dryly and looked at *Bambe* Sams who responded as though they had anticipated the question.

"It is not like that, but it is the same," he said. "He was not enjoying. A man who is not enjoying is a suffer man. You are now a suffer man," he snapped.

Part Three

'Tis better to be that which we destroy,
Than by destruction dwell in doubtful joy.
(Shakespeare: MACBETH)

Chapter Seventeen

The kidnapping and imprisonment of Chopchair which had been feared as the most trying part of the venture turned out to be the least arduous and the least disturbing. Because of the very close similarity between Peter Nwolefeck and Chopchair, the former entered the palace without anybody noticing that there was something amiss, except for a few negligible slips. *Bambe* Isaiahs in whose company he arrived had taken his time to hell him exactly what to do. Like on the previous occasions, the Chopchair was returning from school with his new-found comrade, the prince from Small Monje.

In spite of his nervousness, *Bambe* Peters took time to study every aspect of the palace from the gate overlooking the palace grounds. The palace grounds occupied about a full hectare of land heavily fenced with trees of various species. There was a huge gate at the entrance with steps leading up to a cross-bar before descending, a device common amongst the villagers to keep goats and other domestic animals from straying out of the compound.

On either side of the gate was a post bearing carvings of animals, a snake, a tiger and something like a crocodile. Just outside the gate stood a gigantic Nteuh. From the gate you descended some twenty meters into an arena that served for ceremonial ground. To the left and the right as you stepped into the arena there was a carving of a huge snake with a spear piercing through it. A good distance behind and away from each carving a path bordered by small grass lawns led to huts, probably those of the Chief's wives. You crossed the arena to reach the palace building into which you again had to descend through a wide open door. Two stuffed animals, wild cats and the dry head of a buffalo stood on two low corner tables. From the door, you passed through the *lemo'o*, a large hall. There was a shelf in the far corner on which five skulls were kept. These, the Chief would say later, were the skulls of his dead parents. Two python skins, each measuring at least five metres in length spanned two walls of the *lemo'o*.

From the *lemo'o* you descended again towards the left into the chief's apartment. From the apartment the chief could climb to the veranda of the *lemo'o* through a back passage. This was the passage through which his wives passed to visit him at night. There was a similar passage to the left to the back yard.

From the chief's apartment you descended onto farmyard: an orchard of guavas, oranges, papaws and the like; a garden of plantains, garden eggs and tomatoes. To the back of the farmyard was a palm and raffia bush from which the chief tapped his wine and oil. There was a piggery, a poultry, a small fishpond and some four or five beehives.

***

There were very many important lessons to be learnt, quite apart from the physical environment. When they caught Chopchair and dragged him away to their hide-out, the *Bambe*s feared nobody. Because of the practice exercise they had enacted, they knew that their action was not going to attract undue attention. They did not have any rules to adhere to, except those they had divided for themselves.

As far as they were concerned, whatever worked best was bound to be the best. As soon as the Chopchair was secure in their grip, they expected *Bambe* Peters to stroll

68

effortlessly into the palace, sit in the Chopchair's Chair, kill the Chief if he dared to interfere, declare himself the new chief, order them to kill Chopchair, name his own government and invite them to come into the palace and assume their new roles in the kingdom.

The reality, however, was different. It was completely and painfully different. By virtue of their wild an untutored village upbringing, they all unaware of the fact that in every palace, the princes had a prescribed code of conduct which everybody in the palace knew very well. Whether a prince deserved the title or not depended on how well he kept the rules of conduct.

In Fuo Akendong's palace, for example, from when the heir-apparent was as young as three, children as well as grown ups were used to greeting him in a particular manner. They too expected, and were used to seeing him respond in a particular manner. Children never turned and rebuked them without answering the greeting. Adults greeted him bowing down and clapping their hands three times. The prince was under no obligation to respond. In fact, irrespective of their ages, the people of the palace considered it a favour if the prince responded to their greetings.

On his part, the prince was trained to behave with absolute condescension towards everybody else (including even his own mother), except, of course, Fuo Akendong himself. But even the chief himself, after a sip of his closely guarded WHISKY BLACK, had been known to call the prince Chopchair.

Chapter Eighteen

These were secret conventions of the palace which neither Peter Nwolefeck nor his *Bambe*s were conversant with. When they tied Chopchair's hands and ordered *Bambe* Peters to go into the palace and take over the throne, it did not occur to them that there was still very much to learn. True to their natures and upbringing, they saw Chopchairs arrest and *Bambe* Peters' entering into the palace as the end of their troubles.

Peter Nwolefeck was the very first person to notice that it was just the beginning. Although he shocked everybody by greeting first as he entered the palace with *Bambe* Isaiahs, the entering in itself did not raise any alarm. His troubles, however, began that very night. Chopchair's room, according to the tradition, was separated from the Chief's by a very thin wall. As if in a dream, the chief had overheard the Chopchair ask such questions as "Where did you say the latrine was?" "How did you say greet my father?" and the like.

Early in the morning, some women leaving for the farm had been surprised to hear Chopchair greet them the way their own children did. Even most scandalous was the fact that Chopchair had been sighted urinating from the veranda below which a path led to the main gate from the back of the palace. Although this was a very rare spectacle, and although the Chief heard a few noises about the matter, it did not call for immediate concern. Not even the fact that he had, most unusually, gone to bed without saying good night in the traditional manner to the Chief.

Peter Nwolefeck had spent the entire night wrestling with the problem of not just how to integrate himself into the life if the palace, but to do so the way princes do. He wondered whether he was not better off with his *Bambe*s than in the palace with the strange creatures and strange behaviour patterns which were making him more and more miserable. As he tossed himself from side to side in the palace bed, he imagined his comrades enjoying themselves playing games and conversing in their bamboo beds back in Nzenawung village.

In his uneasiness, the entire mission seemed a lot more displeasing than he had ever conceived. He imagined with a lot of envy, Chopchair sleeping peacefully in his chains, since nobody expected any peculiar behaviour from him. He would wonder for how long his comrades would keep Chopchair, and how they would be feeding him when his own future was so doubtful. He wondered for how long he would live in that state of uneasiness and uncertainty.

He had come to succeed his father, the Chief. But when he looked at the man he looked so strong that he did not think he would live long enough in the palace to await his death in order to take over his throne. The man did not look dieable by any means. He wondered whether the easiest way to succeed the old man was not to kill him and become Chief at once.

Whereas Chopchair could be very easily forced to adapt to the village life of his captivity, Peter Nwolefeck would need all the genius of his life to adapt to the new situation. That needed time and careful planning which they did not have at the time. If he were a new chief of the legal and accepted heir-apparent, he could with time come to learn the responsibilities of this office. But his lack of familiarity with the palace so embarrassed him that he saw an urgent need to return to his wild life in the village. These thoughts so bothered him that he decided he was sick and asked *Bambe*

Isaiahs to inform the Chief about it. He knew more than anybody else, that he was a pretender, an impostor who needed to conceal his true identity, and who needed the shortest possible time to master the ways of the palace. That was difficult.

There was another worry: Rosa could come to the palace and cause him to be betrayed. An idea struck him: he would compel the chief to divide the kingdom between him and Chopchair and give his own share.

Chapter Nineteen

As God would have it, Peter Nwolefeck's absurd behaviour accidentally hastened a solution to the crisis. It began with the fact that the Chief completely misjudged his queer mannerisms. As was common in all the other villages, superstition was a way life with the people of Betaranda. Any form of abnormal behaviour was instantly ascribed to some witch craft. Therefore, when the Chief noticed the strangeness in his Chopchairs's behaviour, he immediately saw the hand of the devil at work. He suspected everybody, especially the other women who had never borne him a son. He immediately suspected the neighbouring Chiefs, whom he thought had used wizardry to destroy his successor so as to appropriate his land after death. It was in this frame of mind that he summoned Ngwika.

"Some enemy of mine has bewitched my son," he said after some time. He named Chief Kujong, Chief Angon and even Chief Kweinyu, Ngwika's uncle, as the possible villains. He then proceeded to describe the ridiculous comportment of the boy to his wife.

"We have to go to ngambe," he declared. Whenever he made such a declaration, it was not open to discussion. But, at any rate, his wife asked to see the boy himself, so as to make her own assessment of the gravity of the situation.

"Go in there and see for yourself," he pointed in the direction of the room. The Chief himself rose as soon as his wife left to visit her son.

The boy was holding his head in his hands and brooding with his palms supporting his jaws. But even from the sitting position, without looking at his face, Ngwika felt her heart leapt to her mouth.

"Look at what the wizards have done to my Chopchair," he said, turning away. Just then something unusual took place. When Peter Nwolefeck looked up into his mother's face she could no contain the shock of discovery.

"Weh!" she shouted.

'Sssshhhh!" Peter Nwolefeck put his finger to his lips warning her to keep quiet. The Chief was a few steps behind the woman, and so did not quite know what had happened. He, however, heard her scream.

"What is the matter?" he enquired

Quickly recollecting herself, she lied:

"Achiebio, you mean that when I see something happening to my child I should not cry?"

The Chief did not respond.

The woman was startled chiefly because she was completely unaware of the presence of any other prince in the palace than Chopchair and his friend.

"We must look for a solution immediately," he told his wife. Ngwika was hardly listening. She could only guess what would happen as soon as the chief discovered that the boy he was beholding was not his Chopchair!

"Achiebio, we must go to ngambe as you say," she said in a voice that was not her own. "I have heard of cases of this nature before, Achiebio. There is somebody I know of who lives in Nzenawung who can treat it. Send me to him."

"We must go to him at once," Fuo-Akendong said.

"No, let me go there first, Achiebio and make sure that he is there and that he will treat Chopchair before we go together."

"Yes," Fuo-Akendong agreed. "You will go alone. And let me have the reply before the sun goes down tomorrow."

As soon as the Chief returned to the veranda Ngwika sneaked back into the room.

"My son, you have come to let us all die?"

"Nobody will die," the boy said. He could have said more, but they heard the Chief's footsteps and abandoned the talk.

76

Chapter Twenty

That same night Ngwika drew Nkem-Fuo and Eshuo Fuo aside and told them:

"We are betrayed. We are dead. Do you know that boy sleeping in there calling himself Chopchair?"

Eshuo-Fuo's heart seemed to miss a beat.

"Is it not Chopchair?" Nkem-Fuo asked.

She told him who he was. Referring to the close resemblance between the brothers, the old man enquired: "My child, how is it possible for me to tell the difference between two drops of water?"

The two men and the woman then proceeded to ask about the line of action to take. Once again there was the big question: "If the son in the palace was not Chopchair, where was chopchair himself?"

"That is what I am going to know from my sister," she told Nkem-Fuo.

Peter Nwolefeck told the Chief that he would not talk to anybody until his mother had returned from the trip.

***

Nzenawung was a good six kilometres from the palace and it took her five hours of toil and tumble to get there. Rosa was at home. Her heart jumped when she saw her sister.

"What is the matter that you look so pale?" she asked Ngwika.

Ngwika did not respond. Instead she enquired in the same worried manner:

"Where is Peter Nwolefeck?"

"Since Peter's voice changed do I see him again? I tell you that, that child will put a rope around my neck one day."

"So where is he?" Ngwika repeated her question.

"Five days today I have not seen him."

Ngwika took a very long breath and, with lips trembling and eyes reddening, she said:

"That is what has brought me here. Peter Nwolefeck is in the palace."

"Don't tell me that..."

"If what I am saying is a lie, let me cut my tongue into three pieces," she swore and then with her heart beating so fast that it made her breathing difficult, she went on: "Achiebio does not know he is the one. He is pretending to be sick, since he is not behaving like Chopchair..."

"Where is Chopchair?" Rosa asked.

The woman threw her hands into the air helplessly.

"Only God alone knows," she said.

"If it is Peter Nwolefeck who is in the palace, what has happened to Chopchair?" Rosa enquired. "I don't want to believe what my heart is trying to tell me, that Peter Nwolefeck has done something terrible to him."

Ngwika shook her head in speechless silence, tears stinging her eyelids.

"That devil like that," Rosa resumed. "He can do anything. His own fire is more that that of Fuo-Akendong himself."

"My sister," she called. "If you noticed this, why did you have to wait for me to come here? Why did you not even send somebody to come for me so that you and I could look for a solution together without involving Achiebio?"

"If you blame me, sister, I will accept the blame.

Our people say that if we are making peace during a war we should not be counting the corpses," she said. "But you have to know what kind of child we are dealing with. You are talking about a child who will listen to you. You are talking about a child who will want you to listen to him. A child who sleeps out every other day, and dares you to ask him a question about his conduct."

The two women decided to return to the palace together and question the boy about his brother. Since the truth had been uncovered there was little to hide any more. They only needed to plan how to explain and plead for clemency; something they knew very well was not possible with the Chief.

Chapter Twenty One

*B*ambe Peters on his part was not sleeping. He told *Bambe* Isaiahs that as soon as his mother returned he would bring everybody together and reveal the truth in such a manner that nobody would suffer. Thus when Ngwika came back with her sister Fuo-Akendong invited them to tell him about their findings. Everybody knew how anxious he was about the health of his successor.

Just then Peter Nwolefeck came in and announced that he wanted to talk to the Chief – alone. All attempts by the women and even the Chief's advisers to dissuade him by luring him into private conversation failed.

"I will only talk to anybody else after I shall have talked to my father," he insisted. So saying he entered the Chief's presence. He asked the Chief to shut the door. He did. He braced himself, knowing that this was the moment of his life, the moment which will make him a Prince or a corpse.

"Father, whom do you think that I am?" he asked coldly but firmly.

The Chief was totally unprepared for the shock that awaited him. Assuming that it was his son's sickness that was making him ask such questions, Fuo-Akendong smiled to himself and shook his head, saying to himself: "when the Gods will destroy a person, they first drive him mad. Is this sickness or madness?"

"No answer me, father. I know that you people have supposed that I am behaving like this because I am sick."

The man blinked his eyes and looked at the boy as if seeing him for the first time. "But are you not sick?" he asked.

"I am not sick. I ask you again, whom do you think that I am?"

When the Chief would not answer he went on:

"I want you to know that I am not Nchonganyi, your Chopchair."

The Chief's face contorted into lines of absolute perplexity. It began to dawn on Fuo-Akendong that there was something strange about him.

"So who are you, then?"

"I am Peter Nwolefeck, the twin brother of Nchonganyi, your Chopchair."

The Chief rubbed his eyes hard, drew in three long breaths, and looked into the boy's face. There, implanted was not sickness but outrage.

"Ngwika!" he shouted as if waking from a bad dream.

When she answered he ordered: "Drag your corpse here." He then called for Nkem-Fuo and Eshuo-Fuo in the same fiery tone. Instead of Ngwika, Nkem-Fuo and Eshuo-Fuo, four persons came in. the fourth was Rosa.

He pulled the two women by their shoulders one by his left and the other by his right hand, and virtually threw them on a bench in the corner. He used his left index finger to show Nkem-Fuo where to sit.

"Have I been dancing with burst drums?" he enquired. "I want you people to hear this and tell me what it all means." He asked the boy to repeat his disclosure. When he finished talking Ngwika who had been sobbing all along burst into tears. The Chief rose to the wall and pulled down spear.

"Shut up that your anus and answer," he barked. "I should be the one to shed tears, not you. Nkem, are you hearing this?"

The old man remained guiltily silent. He looked at the boy. His countenance remained unmoved.

"Where I my Chopchair?" he asked Peter Nwolefeck.

He did not answer. He rose and as he charged at the boy he was frightened by the fact he did not seem scared. Then, that split second it occurred to him that unless he went about it prudently he may lose both boys. Presently the boy confirmed these fears: "My brother, your Chopchair, is a prisoner and you may never see him unless...." He swallowed and kept quiet.

Fuo Akendong was not exactly sure of the particular feelings that seize him. Whereas he was stunned by the young man's boldness and defiance, somewhere at the back of his mind the Chief found something to admire in him. There had to be a strong element of truth in what he was beholding. There had to be something of him in the lad, something which he had always lamented that his Chopchair lacked.

While he sat staring at the boy, mystified, the thought came instantly to his mind of an event which took place many decades ago. On that occasion, his father Fuo-Akendong I had decided that one of his wives, Ndenmengwi, must leave the palace because she was said to have been unfaithful. Ndenmengwi was Akendong's mother. There was proof to the contrary and it was evident that the other wives had framed the story to discredit the woman and so limit the chances of her son becoming Chief in future.

Akendong was not quite sixteen yet, but with his two elder sisters he went up to their father the Chief and forced him to withdraw the threat. The three of them vowed to commit suicide, should their mother be sent away. This was the incident that caused him to leave Betaranda and go to live with an uncle at Penamboko until the death of his father. As his people would say, he seemed now to be receiving a taste of his own medicine. And how bitter the medicine was!

Chapter Twenty Two

"I want you to confirm that what I am hearing is not a nightmare but the living truth," he said to Ngwika. There was nothing else to do. In between sobs she confessed the act.

"Who else knows of this?" he asked, shaking with disbelief.

The woman turned and looked in the direction of Nkem-Fuo and his comrade.

The Chief adjusted the folds of his loin cloth and stuck between his legs, clenched his fist, gnawed at his lips and said:

"Nkem-Fuo, Eshuo-Fuo, is this devil saying that you are not ignorant of this stab in my chest?"

"We will explain, Achiebio," the old men entreated.

"You will not," he shouted. "Nobody will explain why he has to kill me. Nobody."

He rose and charged like a mad bull from hut to hut. He dragged three women he could find, slapped and kicked them until they entered his sitting room. One of them even entered half-naked. When they had been bundled into the room, and without saying anything he dashed into his bedroom, and soon returned with his Dane gun. When Nkem-Fuo attempted to intercept him the Chief knocked him to the ground with the butt.

Fuo Akendong loaded the gun. Everybody sat paralysed with fear. He stepped out, marched into the arena and fired into the trees at the gate, bringing down half the branches. As he was coming back in one of his dogs ran up to him wagging its tail and barking. Holding the barrel of the gun he swung the butt which struck the dog in the muzzle. It fell down, wailing in pain, bleeding. Then, entering the house he addressed his frozen prisoners:

"Our people say you cannot see the anus of a fowl unless the wind is blowing. I have called you all here to tell you what you know about me already: I do not like shame. But you have all managed to do just that to me. I have been shamed not just by Ngwika, but by every single man and woman in this palace because they all knew what was hidden from me. And no doubt, when I stand and strike my chest that I am the only cock to crow in this palace you hold your heads down and smile. And why not smile when you see my anus from behind?

"Before I do what I want to do to everybody who has a hand in this shame that has been brought on me, listen carefully: if there is any woman sitting here who has hidden her own sons so as to use to put me to greater shame one day, let that woman stand up now and talk or be forever silent. If she doesn't and dares some day to mention such bad luck to me, this gun shall tear her into as many pieces as there are leaves on those branches which I have brought down."

"What do you want done?" he turned to Peter Nwolefeck who seemed completely unmoved by all that the Chief was doing. He even seemed to relish it. "We do not settle the price of a rat mole while it is still in the hole! I ask you this cut throat, what do you want done? And where is my Chopchair?"

Peter Nwolefeck took his time and said very slowly:

"You will only see your Chopchair if you…"

"If I do what?

"If you bring you sub-chiefs together…"

"Me, bring who together, for what?"

"We cannot be moving away from bees without throwing the honey combs," Eshuo-Fuo said. "Let Achiebio hold his tongue and give this boy time to talk."

"Whom are you calling a boy? A serpent enters my house…" he checked himself. "Anyway, let him vomit as he wills," the chief said with grim resignation.

Once again, Peter Nwolefeck seemed unmoved beyond his age. Something which hurt and frightened the Chief all the more. He allowed the Chief enough time to shout and them he continued unperturbed:

"The Chief will bring together all his sub-chiefs, swear before them by Ku-Ngang, that for as long as he lived, he will never cause any harm to happen on my mother, my aunt, Nkem-Fuo and everybody else that caused me to be sent to suffer for fifteen years…?"

He looked across at the Chief. The latter spat and ground his teeth.

"And then, and then," he stammered. "And then he will divide this kingdom which he wanted to give to one person, his Chopchair. He will divide the kingdom into two equal halves, between the two of us, his two sons who were born on the same day. After he shall have shown the Chiefs, his Nkem and his Eshuo-Fuo my own half, I shall order his Chopchair to be released and brought here."

Chapter Twenty Three

Fuo Akendong farted in his seat.

"Let it end here," the Chief told Nkem. "A fowl will not grow teeth in my palace. Let he hear no more." He held Nkem's hand and like sleep-walkers, the two men went once more into the room. There he showed Nkem where to sit. With panic written all over his face he preceded:

"Nkem-Fuo, what exactly did I do wrong? What did I do so wrong that you will see somebody stabbing me and remain silent? Please tell me."

"When, Achiebio?"

"I mean when these children were delivered. Why did you people make a fool of me?"

"Your temperament, Achiebio," he said. "Your temperament," he repeated.

"What is wrong with my temperament?" he asked flaring up once more, his voice pitched high in indignation. He struck Nkem-Fuo with the back of his left hand and asked: "What is wrong with my temper?"

The old man rubbed his jaw with his right palm: when the chief repeated the question, he stammered:

"When a lizard nods its head, it doesn't mean that it is always happy." Eshuo-Fuo said in mild reproof. "It looks like when Achiebio does many of these things he does not notice them?"

"Like what things?"

"Achiebio has just struck me...'

"Is that what you call my temperament?"

"No, Achiebio."

"In any case, I asked you a question. Why did you people not tell me?"

"Before Achiebio struck me…"

"I did not strike you. Do you not know when somebody is joking?"

The old man smiled faintly, shook his head and said:

"When Achiebio takes offence at everything that is said and done, people fear to tell him the truth. And as you know, many truths are not usually sweet in the ear."

Fuo Akendong held his head in his hand and reflected for a long time. Then he threw up his head and asked:

"You, as my shadow, what do you suggest that I do? Do you think that boy out there is serious?"

"Achiebio, I do not know him much, but he looks like somebody to fear. Let us listen to him and see how we can mend the past. It is wine that has spilled; let us not break the calabash."

"When you say we listen to him, what exactly do you mean?"

There was no immediate answer. Nkem-Fuo was still reflecting on what to say when the chief lowered his voice and said:

"I do not believe my eyes; I do not believe my ears. I do not believe even in myself. Tell me in one word what should I do?"

"Do exactly as he wants, Achiebio. Let us no hide a calabash in the bush and throw stones there."

"By which you mean that I expose my anus in the market? That I call the same wolves who are waiting to devour my property to come and see what a fool my wives and my children have made of me? That I divide my kingdom while I am still alive? That they refer to Fuo Akendong as a former Chief? Is that what you want me to do? On my dead body!"

Nobody knew better than Nkem-Fuo that nothing frightened Fuo Akendong more than the thought of any fraction of his kingdom ever passing into the hands of the sub-chiefs. With this knowledge at the back of his mind, he said:

"It will be better to do as he says, Achiebio, than allow this animal to kill Chopchair, kill you, kill his mother, kill me and still own the entire kingdom. It will be better than to allow this land to pass into the hands of your labourers who now call themselves chiefs. Your kingdom in the hands of two sons, Achiebio, especially that snake sitting in there, will have a lot more protection than...."

The Chief spat again and clenched his fists.

"Whom is the viper calling chiefs?" he asked furiously. "Empty headed swines to whom I gave titles? Do they have land? I invite landless dogs to come and divide my land?" He seized the old man's hand and dragged him away back into the sitting room. As soon as they re-entered, and as if the two men had been talking about something else, the Chief asked abruptly:

"What if I do not do that?"

Eshuo-Fuo intervened again: "Let us not call a dog with a whip in hand."

"Shut up!? The chief shouted. "I repeat, what if I do not do that?"

"Then you will never see your Chopchair," Peter Nwolefeck said softly but decisively. "Then I will not mind I will not mind what happens to my mother. Then I will not mind what happens to my anus. Then I will not mind what happens to me, nor to you my father."

The chief looked from Nkem-Fuo to Eshuo-Fuo and then to the boy with a mixture of admiration and dread. It was then that it occurred to him that the women were all there, listening, watching.

"Disappear from here," he ordered them out of his presence. "Witches all," he cursed as he shut the door behind the last one. He sat quiet for a very long time, holding his face in his hands. Whom was he going to trust? He could not trust his closest advisers, he could not trust any of his wives. He could not tell how many pieces he would eventually have to divide his kingdom. He did not know what else was being hidden from him. He did not know whether as soon as the kingdom was divided in the two princes would not team up and kill him.

"Death has broken the shoulder on the spot where my bag hangs," he sighed. "I will not be party to the nonsense," he told Nkem-Fuo. "Get in touch with those cut-throats you call Chiefs. Let the leeches come tomorrow morning and cut me up into pieces, let them suck as much as they have always wanted for themselves. Let them give the rest to the devil and his disciple."

Epilogue

As a matter of fact, Fuo Akendong was no party to the division of his kingdom. He was not there although he authorised his elders to execute the order. He died that same night of heart failure! But the death was not announced until the division of the land had taken place. Peter Nwolefeck was given half the kingdom. The other half went to Chopchair. As soon as his own share had been shown to him he dispatched *Bambe* Isaiahs to take the good news back to his comrades and ask them to lead Chopchair back to the palace.

It was further arranged that the two princes would rule in turns: one would rule for two years and then the other would take over. It was decided that for convenience Peter Nwolefeck would rule first. But it seemed unlikely that he would ever allow his brother to rule because immediately that decision was taken, *Bambe* Peters was overheard murmuring to his *Bambe*s:

"A man rules for fifteen years but when it comes to my own turn to chop they say two years. I will see the fire that will send me out of this chair of rule."

The End